Le S. Elf

(The S. Elf)

Lyle & Joany Erickson

le S. Elfe

The S. Elf

228 Hamilton Ave.,
Palo Alto, CA 94301

ISBN 978-1-960946-19-5 (softcover)
ISBN 978-1-960946-20-1 (ebook)

This book is a work of fiction. Names, characters, places, and incidents are the product of the author's imagination or are used fictitiously. Any resemblance to actual locales, events, or persons, living or dead, is purely coincidental.

Printed in the United States of America.

*Le S. Elf (*Luh Ess Elf*) lived in a small, blue pond.

From which he NEVER.... EVER ventured beyond.

He lived, by himself, all.... alone there.

For with others Le S. Elf refused to share.

*The Elf

Bubble-Bubble, Glug-Glug.

Sang Le S. Elf so smug

As he gave himself a hug.

For him there was no "you and me".

No friends... no family.

He thought that if he were
alone he would be happy.

In his heart, to himself,
he cried..."Whoopee"!

All alone, by
himself, was he.

In this small, blue pond
he called a sea.

This is the way he
wanted things to be.

Bubble-Bubble, Glug-Glug.
Sang Le S. Elf so smug.

As he gave himself a hug.

One day....

A *Tortue de mer (*tur-tue duh mare*) came to stay.

Turtle moved.... very.... very slow.

He sank to the bottom of the pond.... deep.... down.... low.

Like a mossy, old rock Tortue de mer did lay.

He had no desire for games of frolic or play.

Staying in the cool, deep water was what really made his day.

*Turtle

Le S. Elf gave a ferocious, fish-bubble gurgle.

His scales darkened, becoming a most annoying shade of purple.

A real thug at heart, he had been waiting so he could act tough.

He was certainly bad enough to be mean and rough.

Fiercely he huffed.

Savagely he puffed.

He knew he could call any other critter's bluff. "T...h...i...i...s...s...s...s is MY pond.

Of you, Mr. Turtle, I am far less than fond.

Don't.. .you.. .dare.. .stay!

Tortue de mer.-.you must...you must....**Go away.**"

Le S. Elf continued to bellow his most ferocious and loudest fish shout.

Telling poor, dowdy, old turtle how much he wanted him...OUT!

"Must I say it again... TURTLE... that you have to go?

Aha...then... let it be so! Turtle... I say...you really are very stupid and slow.

Now, turtle...don't...you...dare...give me no trouble.

Get out of here.. .stupid.. .slow one...on the double."

Poor Tortue de mer.

His tender heart became filled with a sudden, cold fear.

So.. .shedding.. .many.. .a.. .big.. .salt-tear,

Old mossy-rock turtle immediately departed.

All very sad and broken-hearted.

He went out into the cold and cruel

"Big Beyond."

Far and away from a cozy home

in the small blue pond.

A bright, shiny, green *Grenoille (*gra new yah*) hopped.

You might say.. .he more or less.. .from out of the sky...dropped.

Whatever you choose to call it...at his coming he really just sort of...ker-plopped!

When into the pond he came with a bold, green dash.

Frog's sudden, unexpected, humongous crash

Was such a pond-shattering splash

That it made Le S. Elf's heart skip and fade

Just a thump...thump...thumpity...tad shade.

Le S. Elf curled his thin fish lips.

He even did a couple

of fast fish flips,

Tumbling right over

his own fine, fishy fin.

What a terrible fish

fit...this fish...

did fall in.

*Frog

With a loud bubble-glug yell

That certainly did not sound at all well,

Le S. Elf chased green frog away...

Pell-mell

"Ooohh, swell!" Croaked gentleman frog

As he hopped out onto a log.

He would never be one to insist that he be allowed to stay.
But he was rather 'unsettled' at being told to go away.

And it was true, he realized,

That to this pond, as yet, he had no family ties.

Also...and most importantly...in the ways of
the water world he was rather wise.

Grenoille was far too smart...and in no mood...

To become FISH FOOD!!!!

Indeed, without waiting to even stop,

Except, of course, for that first...

big...splash ker-plop.

Proper...as proper
could be...

away went frog
in one, quick...

green blur
of a hop.

A wind-blown *Demoiselle (*dem wa zell*) fluttered down upon the blue pond next.

Her gentle landing, or course, caused Le S. Elf to become

all...blow-bubbly, vexed.

The shimmering glory of her rainbowed wings

Did not cause the fish to think of pleasant, well-meaning things.

*Dragon fly

Le S. Elf was such a hostile lout.

Once again, in...HIS...pond, he swirled all about.

Then he began that same tired, old, loud, fish shout.

"Out! Out! Out! This is my pond! Of that, there can be no doubt!

Therefore, you must fly out!... Out! Out!"

Le S. Elf created such a combative hue and cry.

Away...away...sailed Demoiselle, soft as a summer sigh.

Her appreciation for peace and love were so very high.

Sad, but, in this small, blue pond they did not seem to lie.

She had her standards.

She would rather do than die.

And since, with those who made war,

she would not vie,

She being more the lover...

less the fighter...oh my!

That being that...Away...away...gentle Demoiselle did fly.

A little, lame, white *Canard (*can nard*) quacked a happy
quack as she waddled into the small blue pond.

You see, ducks and water have a mutual and natural bond.

They go together, like birds of a feather.

The blue pond water tickled the toes on ducks web-footed feet.

"Oh! Wonderful, wonderful water! So wet and so sweet.

Of you, dearest friend, I am so very, very fond.

I think that I shall love living here on this small, blue pond."

*Duck

"This pond.-.'Tis mine, 'Tis mine, Tis mine,"

Gurgled Le S. Elf with an irritating, bubbly-fish whine.

Such a fish-bully swagger.

Like a mean-mouthed bragger.

With a great deal of self-righteous anger,

Le S. Elf nipped a pretty, white feather

right out of little, lame duck's tail.

Off and away, in that web-footed waddle, hobbled duck

through the mud and muck

With a timid "Quack" and a sad, alarmed wail.

A laughing, freckle-faced *Garconnet (*gar so nay*) made a

GREAT BIG red-headed splash when he dived in.

This put Le S. Elf on the spot.

The fish was not at all that hot

About letting him, an actual, real live, human boy stay for a swim!

At first Le S. Elf tried to scare the boy with a bubble-glug fish bluff.

Then, of course, when that did not work, he got a little rough.

You see Le S. Elf always had to be the one to win.

But the boy, being a boy, would never let something with a fin do him in.

*Boy

"Well, look at that!

What a fish!

So big! So fat!

Fish, don't do that!

Be good.

Like a regular fish should.

Or, you could end up a fish...

dish!"

Le S. Elf simply...could...not...stand it.

He really had a big, fish fit.

Le S. Elf was in such a terrible peeve.

Still...

the boy absolutely...

positively, refused to leave.

To Le S. Elf it did not seem at

all...right.

So...

he gave the boy a horrible,

nasty fish bite.

Right on...on Red-head's toe.

Oh!...Oh!...Oh!

That is a...No!...No!...No!

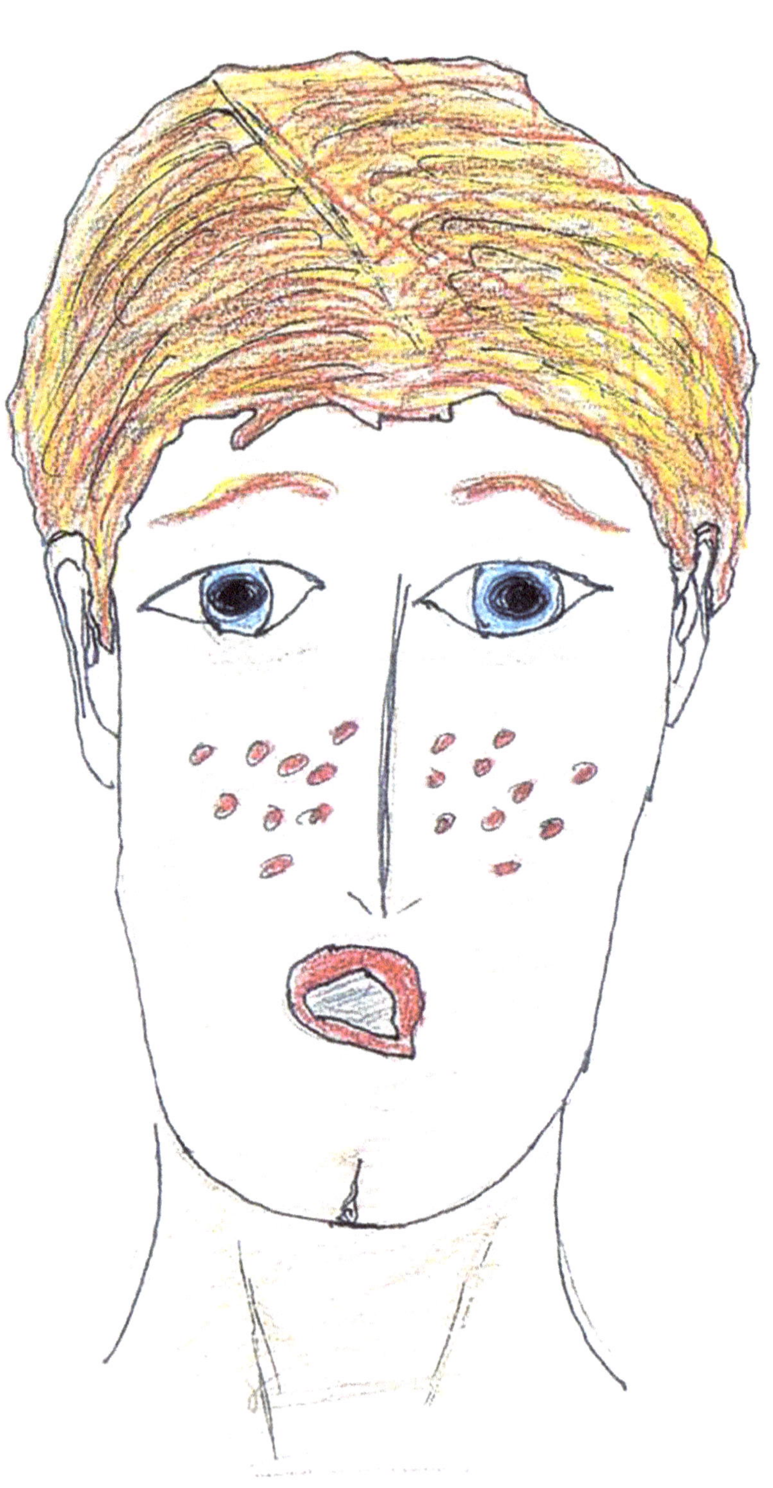

"Oh...oh...oh...Gross fish!

It is not my wish

to kick up a water-war storm.

But that really was...in bad form."

He admonished Le S. Elf in startled surprise.

Then the offended boy, from the small, blue pond did arise.
Affirming to the fish...that...which you and I have already surmised.
"You, Mr. Fish, are a most wicked and improper grouch!"

The boy refused to utter even one little Ouch! Ouch! Ouch!
The Garconnet was not one to snivel and moan.

Bravely, clutching his wound, Red-head departed for home.

Later that very same day,

A red-headed, freckle-faced *pecheur (*pesh-er*) came by the way.

He dropped in his line-.-.ker-plunk!

To the bottom of the small, blue pond it sunk.

"I can not be had.

I do not fight.

I do not get mad.

I can make it right."
The boy smiled under
his big straw hat.
"Well fish tht's that!"

*Fisherman

20

Le S. Elf, in a fast swirl

Did a complete, triple-turn twirl.

What a mean,

Unclean,

Monstrous rotter

The fish, all alone, had become...in the blow-bubbly water.
Swimming frantically around...and around;

Searching angrily until that *Larve (*larv*) on the hook he found.

*Worm

Spitting out great gobs of bubbly foam.

Raging because he wanted to be left all alone.

Making a freakish fish-squeal,

One with lots of frenzied fish-zeal.

Le S. Elf shouted...as rude...as rude

could ever think to be.

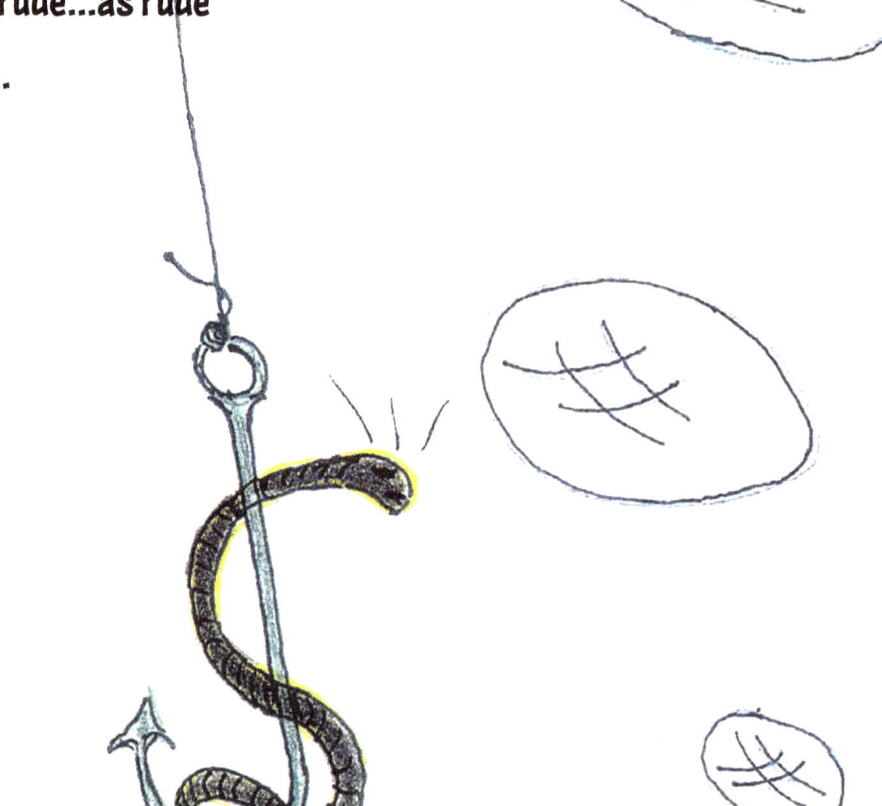

"Go worm! Go from MY sea!"

The worm squirmed. The worm turned.

The worm sighed.

"Uh-oh!"

Then the worm bravely replied,

'Well...No!"

Le S. Elf, in a fighting rage-double

Gave out an irritating blow-fish bubble.

That annoying sound of elf-fish trouble.

How overwhelmingly sad.

It is pitifully bad.

To be so grossly mad

That it curls a fish's fin.

 What a sad...bad...mad sin

For any fish to ever fall in.

Le S. Elf bubble-glugged with all his might.

"Hey! I will give you such a fight.

I will give you a great big bite!"

Shark-like he circled around the worm... tight.

"This fighting fish will turn you...

into...

a real tasty worm-dish!"

Le S. Elf then opened his jaws

REAL wide.

All the better to get that

whole...

    worm...

        deep...

           inside.

The worm was small.

More l...o...n...g than tall.

However, he was clever and smart.

At the VERY last instant, he made a quick dart. You
see, the worm also had his bag of tricks.

There wasn't much that worm could not fix.

With a slippery worm-wiggle,

With a super-fast worm-squiggle,

The little worm beat a very hasty retreat.

Too wise was he...

To hang around and be...

Something munchy

and crunchy...

for the fish to eat.

It was the fish that bubbled

an angry cough

When the worm was

suddenly from the hook...

off.

It was a not a juicy worm but the hard, metal hook...

That angry Le S. Elf suddenly took!

When, with a shout of fisherman's joy,

The red-headed, freckle-faced boy,

On his pole gave a yank and pull.

And Le S. Elf got his obnoxious, loud mouth full!

After all has been said and done,

It is a whole lot better and gobs more fun

Down on the small, blue water-world pond.

And...even out there in the big, Big, BIG beyond

Now that Le S. Elf-fish...(THE SELFISH)...is gone.

They all get along.

They sing a happy together-song.

Bubbly-bubble, glug-glug,

Be quick to give another a hug.

When you are willing to share,

There is room and plenty to spare.

May there always be

laughter and mirth

All together, here

on our awesome...

big...blue Earth.

CAST OF CHARACTERS AS THEY APPEAR IN THE STORY:

Le S. Elf (*Luh ess elf*) The S. Elf

ELF: A small, mischievous or malicious creature.

Tortue de mer (*Tortue duh mare*) Turtle

Turtle: Any of an order of land, fresh-water or marine reptiles that has a toothless, bony beak and a bony shell enclosing the trunk and into which the head, limbs and tail can be withdrawn.

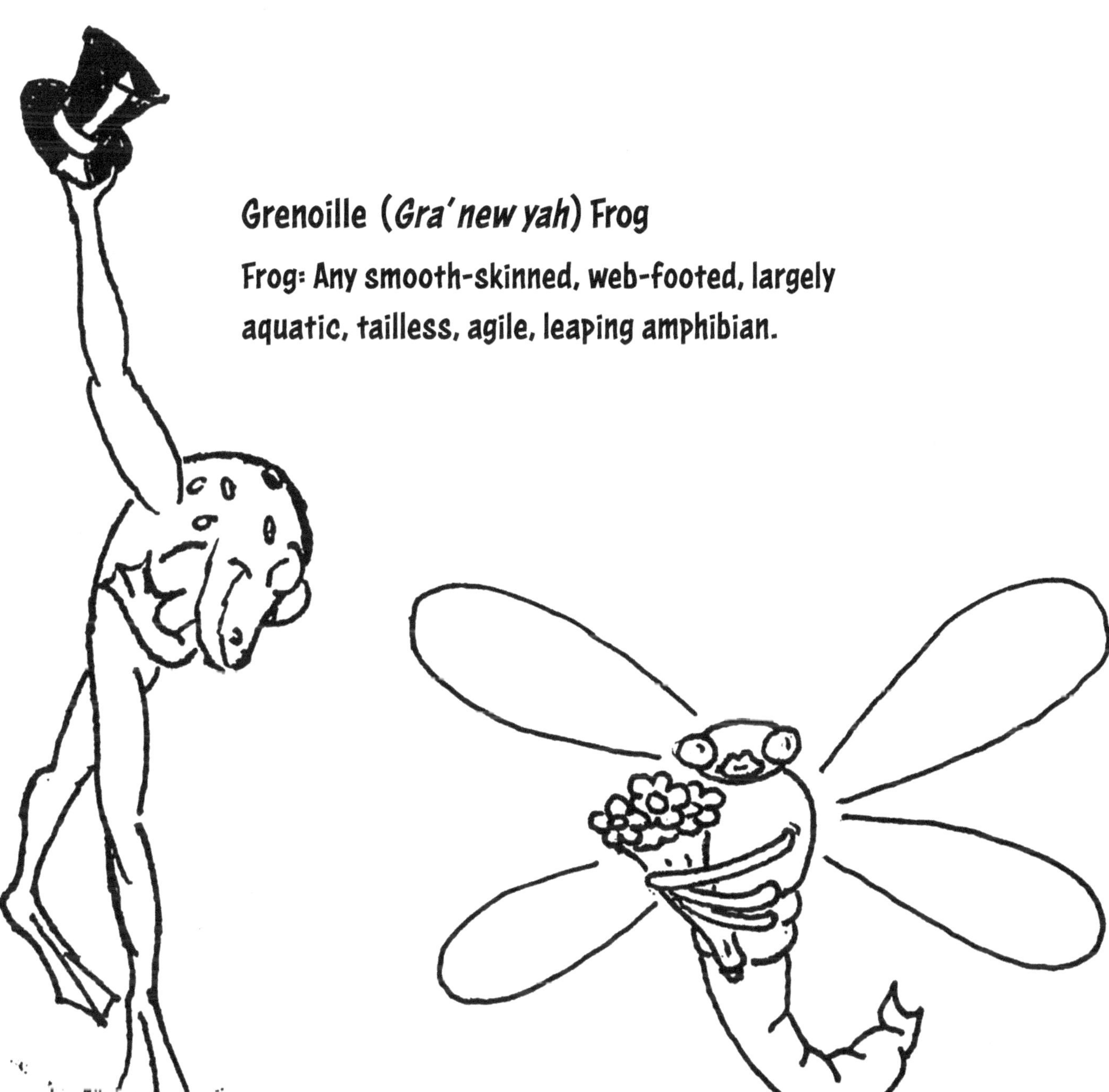

Grenoille (*Gra' new yah*) Frog

Frog: Any smooth-skinned, web-footed, largely aquatic, tailless, agile, leaping amphibian.

Demoiselle (*Dem wa zell*) Dragonfly

Dragonfly: The adult of any member of the suborder anisoptera. They vary in length from a half inch to almost five inches. Some fossil dragonflies which lived a million years ago were a foot long and had a wing-span of two feet.

Canard (*Can nard*) Duck

Duck: Any of various swimming, web-footed birds in which the neck and legs are short, the body depressed and the bill broad and flat.

Garconnet (*Gar so nay*) Boy

Boy: A male child, from birth to puberty.

Pecheur (*Pesh er*)

Fisherman

Fisherman: One who engages in fishing as an occupation or for pleasure.

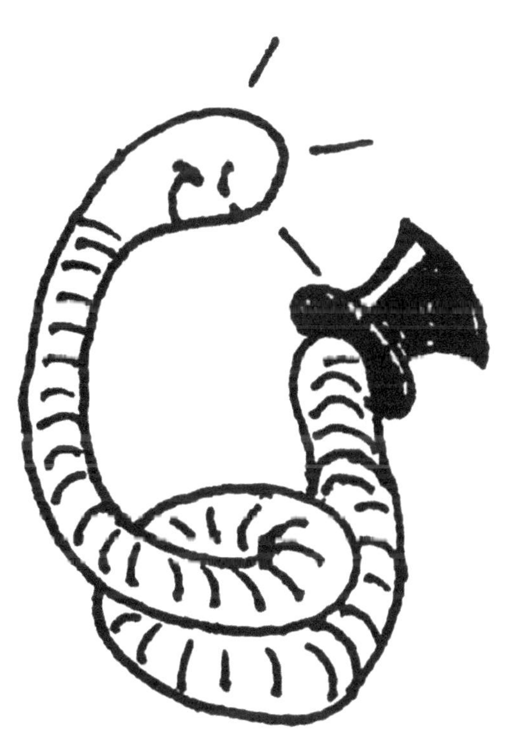

Larve (*Larv*) Worm

Worm: Any of numerous relatively small elongated, naked and soft-bodied animals; as an Earthworm.

Le S. Elf Fish (THE SELFISH)

*TOUCHE (*Too shay*)

THE END